D1139166

Seven Tales

Seven Tales

from

HANS CHRISTIAN ANDERSEN

Illustrations by
VILHELM PEDERSEN
and
LORENZ FRØLICH

Translation by
R. P. KEIGWIN

HØST & SØN

Seven Tales
Copyright © 1987 & 2003 by Høst & Søn, Copenhagen
2. edition, 2. printing 2005
Cover by Peter Stoltze, stoltzedesign
Paper-cuttings by Hans Christian Andersen according to
aggrement with Odense City Museums
Printed in Denmark by Narayana Press, Gylling 2005

ISBN 87-14-22047-4

I denne serie foreligger eventyr af H.C. Andersen på engelsk, fransk, hollandsk, japansk, kinesisk og tysk. Udvalgene består af: **Engelsk:** Kejserens nye klæder, Nattergalen, Hyrdinden og skorstensfejeren, Den grimme ælling, Gartneren og herskabet, Snemanden, Den lille pige med svovlstikkerne. **Fransk:** Prinsessen på ærten, Nattergalen, Den grimme ælling, Grantræet, Den lille pige med svovlstikkerne, Historien om en moder. **Hollandsk:** Kejserens nye klæder, Nattergalen, Hyrdinden og skorstensfejeren, Den grimme ælling, Snemanden, Den lille pige med svovlstikkerne, Hvad fatter gør, det er altid det rigtige, Prinsessen på ærten, Det er ganske vist! **Japansk:** Den grimme ælling, De røde sko, Nattergalen, Prinsessen på ærten, Svinedrengen. **Kinesisk:** Kejserens nye klæder, Nattergalen, Hyrdinden og skorstensfejeren, Den grimme ælling, Gartneren og herskabet, Snemanden, Den lille pige med svovlstikkerne. **Tysk:** Kejserens nye klæder, Nattergalen, Kærestefolkene, Den standhaftige tinsoldat, Den lille Idas blomster, Den grimme ælling, Den lille pige med svovlstikkerne.

HØST & SØN • KØBMAGERGADE 62 • 1150 KØBENHAVN K
www.hoest.dk

Contents

The Emperor's New Clothes

Many years ago there lived an Emperor who was so tremendously fond of fine new clothes that he spent all his money on being elegantly dressed. He took no interest in his army or the theatre or in driving through the country, unless it was to shew off his new clothes. He had different clothes for every hour of the day and, just as you might say of a King that he was in the council-chamber, so it was always said of the Emperor: »He's in his wardrobe.«

There was plenty of fun going on in the city where

the Emperor lived. Strangers were continually arriving, and one day there came two swindlers. They made out they were weavers and could weave the very finest stuffs imaginable. Not only were colours and design unusually attractive, but the clothes made from their material had the peculiarity of being invisible to anyone who wasn't fit for his post or who was hopelessly stupid.

»I say! They must be wonderful clothes,« thought the Emperor. »If I had some, I could find out which of my statesmen were unfit for their posts and also be able to tell the clever ones from the stupid. Yes, I must have some of that stuff woven for me at once.« And he paid down a large sum of money to the swindlers straight away, so as to enable them to start work.

And they did; they put up a couple of looms and pretended to be working, although there was absolutely nothing in the loom. They coolly demanded the most delicate silk and the finest gold thread, which they promptly stowed away in their own bags; and then they went on working far into the night at their empty looms.

»Well, now, I wonder how they are getting on with the work,« said the Emperor to himself. But there was one point that really made him feel rather anxious, namely, that a man who was stupid or quite unfit for his post would never be able to see what was woven. Not that he need have any fears for himself – he was quite confident about that – but all the same it might be better to send someone else first, to find out how things were going. Everyone in the city had heard of the mysterious power possessed by the material, and they were all eager to discover how incapable or stupid his neighbour was.

»I'll send my honest old Prime Minister to the weavers',« thought the Emperor. »He's the best one to see what the stuff looks like, for he has plenty of sense and nobody fills his post better than he does.«

So off went the honest old Premier to the workshop where the two swindlers sat busy at their empty looms. »Lor' bless my soul,« thought the Minister with eyes starting out of his head. »Why, I can't see anything!« But he was careful not to say so.

The two swindlers begged him to take a closer look – didn't he find the colours and design most attractive? They then pointed to the empty loom but, although the poor old Minister opened his eyes wider and wider, he couldn't see a thing; for there wasn't a thing to see. »Good Lord!« he thought, »Is it possible that I'm stupid? I never suspected that, and not a soul must hear of it. Can it be that I'm unfit for my post? No, it will never do for me to say that I can't see the material.«

»Well, what do you think of it?« asked the one who pretended to be weaving.

»Oh, it's charming! Quite exquisite!« said the old Minister, looking through his spectacles. »What a pattern and what colouring! I shall certainly tell the Emperor how pleased I am with it.«

»Ah, we're glad to hear that,« said the swindlers, and they then gave details of the colours and the peculiar design. The old Minister listened carefully, so as to be able to repeat all this when he came back to the Emperor – which he duly did.

The swindlers now demanded more money, more silk and more gold thread, for these would be required for weaving. They put it all into their own pockets – not a thread came into the loom – while they went on working the empty frames as before.

By and by, the Emperor sent another honest official to see how the weaving was getting on and whether the stuff wouldn't soon be ready. The same thing happened to him as to the Minister: he looked and looked but, as nothing was there but the empty looms, he couldn't see anything.

»There, isn't it a handsome piece!« said the swindlers, as they pointed out the beauty of the design which wasn't there at all.

»I know I'm not stupid,« thought the man, »so it must be my fine position I'm not fit for. Some people might think that rather funny, but I must take good care they don't get to hear of it.« And then he praised the material which he couldn't see and assured them of his delight in its charming shades and its beautiful design. »Yes, it's quite exquisite,« he said to the Emperor, when he got back.

The splendid material became the talk of the Town. And now the Emperor himself said he must see it while it was still in the loom. Quite a throng of select people, including the two honest old officials who had been there already, went with him to where both the crafty swindlers were now weaving for all they were worth without the vestige of a thread.

»Look, isn't it magnificent!« said the two honest officials. »If Your Majesty will but glance – what a pattern, what colouring!« And they pointed to the empty loom, feeling certain that the others could see the material.

»What's this?« thought the Emperor. »I can't see anything – this is appalling! Am I stupid? Am I not fit to be Emperor? This is the most terrible thing that could happen to me... Oh, it's quite wonderful,« he said to them; »it has our most gracious approval.« And he gave a satisfied nod, as he looked at the empty loom; he wasn't going to say that he couldn't see anything. All the courtiers who had come with him looked and looked, but they made no more of it than the rest had done. Still, they all said just what the Emperor said – »Oh, it's quite wonderful!« – and they advised him to have some clothes made from this splendid new material and to wear them for the first time in the grand procession that was shortly taking place. »Magnificent!« »Delightful!« »Superb!« were the comments that ran from mouth to mouth; everyone was so intensely pleased with it. On each of the swindlers the Emperor bestowed a knighthood, with a badge to wear in his button-hole, and the title of Imperial Weaver.

On the eve of the procession the swindlers sat up all night with something like twenty lighted candles. People could see how busy they were finishing off the

Emperor's new clothes. They pretended to take the stuff off the loom, they clipped away at the air with huge scissors, they worked at their needles without thread, and at last they announced: »There! The Emperor's clothes are ready!«

Then the Emperor, with his most distinguished gentlemen-in-waiting, went in person to the weavers, who each put out his arm just as if he were holding something and said: »Here are the Breeches! Here is the Robe! Here is the Mantle!« And so on. »They are all as light as gossamer; you can hardly feel you have anything on – that's just the beauty of them.«

»Yes, indeed,« answered the gentlemen-in-waiting. But they couldn't see a thing, for there wasn't a thing to see.

»Now will Your Imperial Majesty be graciously pleased to take off your clothes?« said the swindlers. »Then we can fit you with the new ones, there in front of the big glass.«

So the Emperor took off the clothes he was wearing, and the swindlers pretended to hand him each of the new garments they were supposed to have made, and they took him at the waist as if they were fastening something on... it was the train, and the Emperor turned and twisted in front of the looking-glass.

»Goodness! How well they suit your Majesty! What a wonderful fit!« they all exclaimed. »What a cut! What colours! What sumptuous robes!«

The Master of Ceremonies came in with an announcement. »The canopy to be carried above Your Majesty in the procession is waiting outside.«

»All right, I'm ready,« said the Emperor. »Aren't they a nice fit!« And he turned round once more in front of the glass, for he really had to make them think he was gazing at his fine clothes.

The chamberlains who were to carry the train groped about on the floor as if they were picking the train up; and, as they walked, they held out their hands, not daring to let it be thought that they couldn't see anything.

There marched the Emperor in the procession under the beautiful canopy, and everybody in the streets and at the windows said: »Goodness! The Emperor's new clothes are the finest he has ever had. What a wonderful train! What a perfect fit!« No one would let it be thought that he couldn't see anything, because that would have meant he wasn't fit for his job, or that he was very stupid. Never had the Emperor's clothes been such a success.

»But he hasn't got anything on!« said a little child. »Goodness gracious, do you hear what the little innocent says?« cried the father; and the child's remark was whispered from one to the other.

»He hasn't got anything on! There's a little child saying he hasn't got anything on!«

»Well, but he hasn't got anything on!« the people all shouted at last. And the Emperor felt most uncomfortable, for it seemed to him that the people were right. But somehow he thought to himself: »I must go through with it now, procession and all.« And he drew himself up still more proudly, while his chamberlains walked after him carrying the train that wasn't there.

The Nightingale

You know of course that in China the Emperor is a Chinese and his subjects are Chinese too. The story I'm going to tell you happened many years ago, but that's just why you had better hear it now before it's forgotten.

The Emperor's palace was the finest palace in the world, made entirely of delicate porcelain. It was all so precious and fragile that you had to be tremendously careful how you touched anything. The garden was full of the rarest flowers, and the loveliest of these had little silver bells tied to them which tinkled so that no one should go by without noticing them. Yes, everything in the Emperor's garden was most carefully thought out, and it stretched so far that even the gardener had no idea where it ended. If you kept on walking, you found yourself in a glorious wood with tall trees and deep lakes. The wood went right down to the sea, which was blue and deep; big ships could sail right in under the branches of the trees. Here lived a nightingale that sang so beautifully that even the poor fisherman, who had so much else to see to, would stop and listen, when he was taking his nets in at night and suddenly heard the nightingale. "My word! that's lovely!" he said; but then he had to get on with his work and forgot about the bird. Yet when she sang again the following night and the fisherman was out there with his nets, "My word!" he repeated, "that is lovely!"

From every country in the world travellers came and marvelled at the Emperor's great city, his palace and his garden; but as soon as they heard the nightingale, everyone said the same – "Oh, but that's the best of all!" And when they got home from their travels, they had many tales to tell, and clever people wrote books about the city and the palace and the garden, yet they never forgot the nightingale; she was given the place of honour. And the poets wrote the most lovely poems, all about the nightingale in the wood there beside the deep sea.

These books went all over the world, and so in course of time some of them reached the Emperor. There he sat in his golden chair, reading and reading; and now and then he nodded his head, for he was pleased to come across such splendid descriptions of the city and the palace and the garden. "But the nightingale is really the best of all," said the book he was reading.

"What's this?" thought the Emperor. "The nightingale? Why, I've never heard of her! Is there such a bird in my Empire and, what's more, in my own garden? Nobody's ever told me that – one has to read about it in a book!" And, with that, he summoned his gentleman-in-waiting, who was so grand that, whenever anyone of lower rank than himself ventured to speak to him or to ask a question, he only answered "P!" – and that means nothing at all. "It says here that we have a most remarkable bird called a nightingale," said the Emperor. "They declare that there's nothing like her in all my Empire. Why have I never been told of this before?"

"It's the first I've ever heard of her," repeated the gentleman-in-waiting. "She's never been presented at Court."

"I command her to be brought here this evening to sing to me," said the Emperor. "The whole world knows what I possess – and I know nothing!"

"It's the first I've ever heard of her," repeated the gentleman-in-waiting. "I shall look for her, and I shall find her."

Find her? But where? The gentleman-in-waiting ran upstairs and downstairs, through rooms and passages, but none of the people he met had ever heard of the nightingale. So the gentleman-in-waiting hurried once more to the Emperor and said it was obviously a story invented by those who write books. "Your Majesty mustn't believe everything you read. Most of it's just made up – what they call black art."

"But the book I read it in," said the Emperor, "was sent me by the high and mighty Emperor of Japan, so it can't be untrue. I *will* hear the nightingale. She's to come and sing to-night, under my royal patronage; and if she fails to appear, then every courtier shall be punched in the stomach directly after supper."

"Tsing-pe!" said the gentleman-in-waiting and ran up and down all the stairs again, through all the rooms and passages; half the Court ran with him, for they didn't a bit like the idea of being punched in the stomach. They kept asking after this extraordinary nightingale that everybody knew about except the people at Court.

At last they came across a poor little girl in the kitchen, who said "Oh, golly – the nightingale? I know her well. My, how she can sing! Every evening I'm allowed to take home a few scraps from the table for my poor sick mother who lives down by the shore; and on my way back I often take a rest in the wood, and then I hear the nightingale singing. It brings tears to my eyes, just as if my mother were kissing me."

"Little kitchen-maid," said the gentleman-in-waiting, "you shall have a regular situation in the kitchen and be allowed to watch the Emperor eating his dinner, if only you'll take us to the nightingale. You see, she's to give a command performance this evening before the Emperor."

So then they all set out for the wood where the nightingale used to sing; half the Court joined in the quest. As they were going along, a cow began to moo. "Ah, there she is!" said the courtiers. "What remarkable strength in such a small creature! Yes, it's certainly not the first time we've heard her."

"No, but that's a cow mooing," said the little kitchen-maid. "We've still got a long way to go."

Then some frogs started croaking in the pond. "Delightful!" said the Emperor's chaplain. "Now I can hear her: just like little church-bells."

"No, those are frogs," said the little kitchen-maid. "But I expect we shall soon hear her now." And then the nightingale began to sing.

"There she is!" said the little girl. "Listen, listen! There she is, up there" – and she pointed to a little grey bird up in the branches.

"Is it possible?" said the gentleman-in-waiting. "Why, I never pictured her like that. How ordinary she looks! I expect she's off colour through having so many distinguished visitors."

"Little nightingale," called out the small kitchen-maid quite boldly, "our gracious Emperor would like you to sing to him."

"With the greatest of pleasure," said the nightingale, and at once began to sing most deliciously.

"Just like glass bells," observed the gentleman-in-waiting. "And look at the way her little throat keeps working. I can't make out why we've never heard her before. She'll make a great hit at Court."

"Shall I sing once more to the Emperor?" asked the nightingale, for she thought the Emperor was there.

"My excellent little nightingale," replied the gentleman-in-waiting, "it's my very pleasant duty to summon you to a concert this evening at the palace, where you will enchant His Imperial Majesty with your delightful singing."

"It sounds best out in the open," said the nightingale. Still, she went along readily enough on hearing it was the Emperor's wish.

At the palace everything had been polished up, until the china walls and floors glittered in the light of thousands and thousands of gold lamps. The loveliest flowers, hung ready for tinkling, were arranged in the corridors; and there was such a draught from the scurrying to and fro that their bells were all set ringing and you couldn't hear a word that was spoken.

In the middle of the great hall in which the Emperor sat was a golden perch for the nightingale. The entire Court was present; and the little kitchen-maid was allowed to stand behind the door, as she now ranked as a regular palace kitchen-maid. Everyone was dressed in their finest clothes, and they all looked at the little grey bird as the Emperor nodded to her to begin.

And the nightingale sang so beautifully that tears came into the Emperor's eyes and trickled right down his cheeks; and then the nightingale's singing became even lovelier – it went straight to his heart. And the Emperor was so pleased that he said the nightingale should have his gold slipper to wear round her neck; but the nightingale said no thank you, she had been rewarded enough already. "I've seen tears in the Emperor's eyes; that's my richest reward. There's a strange power in an Emperor's tears. Heaven knows, they are reward enough!" And then the nightingale let them hear her lovely voice again.

"Who ever saw such airs and graces!" said the ladies around; and they went and filled their mouths with water so as to gurgle when anyone spoke to them; yes, they thought they could be nightingales too. Even the lackeys and ladies' maids expressed their approval; and that's saying a good deal for they are the most difficult of all to satisfy. There's no doubt whatever, the nightingale made a great hit.

She was now to remain at Court and have her own cage, with leave to go out for two walks in the daytime and one at night. She was given twelve attendants, who each held on tightly to a silk ribbon fastened round her leg. There was absolutely no fun in a walk like that.

The whole city was talking of this remarkable bird, and, when two people met, one of them merely said "night" and the other "gale", and after that they sighed and quite understood each other. What's more, eleven grocer's children were named after her, but not one of them had a note in its head...

One day a large parcel arrived for the Emperor, with the word "Nigthingale" written on the outside.

"I expect this is a new book about our famous bird," said the Emperor. But it wasn't a book at all; it was a little gadget lying in a box – an artificial nightingale that was supposed to look like the live one but was covered all over with diamonds, rubies and sapphires. You only had to wind it up, and it could sing one of the songs that the real nightingale sang; and all the while its tail went up and down, glittering with silver and gold. Round its neck was a little ribbon, on which was written: "The Emperor of Japan's nightingale is poor beside the Emperor of China's."

"How delightful!" they all said; and the one who brought the artificial bird was at once given the title of Chief Imperial Nightingale Bringer.

"Now they must both sing at once," suggested somebody. "What a duet that will be!"

So the two birds had to sing together; but it wasn't a success, because the real nightingale sang in her own way, whereas the artificial bird went by clockwork. "It can't be blamed for that", said the Master of the Emperor's Music. "It keeps perfect time and follows my own methods exactly." After that, the artificial bird had to sing by itself. It was just as popular as the real one, and of course it was also much prettier to look at, glittering there like a cluster of brooches and bracelets.

Over and over again it sang its one and only song – thirty-three times without tiring – and the listeners would have liked to hear it all once more, but the

Emperor thought that now it was time for the real nightingale to do some singing... But where ever was she? No one had noticed her fly out of the open window, away to her own green woods.

"Bless my soul, what's the meaning of this?" said the Emperor; and all the courtiers were highly indignant and said what an ungrateful creature the nightingale was. "Still, we've got the better one," they added; and then the artificial bird was obliged to sing once more. That was the thirty-fourth time they were hearing the same song; but they didn't quite know it even yet, for it was so difficult. And the Master of Music gave the bird extraordinary praise; in fact, he declared that it was better than the real nightingale, not merely because of its outward appearance and all the wonderful diamonds, but also for the work inside.

"You see, ladies and gentlemen and, above all, Your Imperial Majesty, with the real nightingale there's no telling what's going to happen. But with the artificial bird everything is fixed beforehand. Such-and-such will be heard and no other. One can account for it all: one can open it up and show the human mind at work, the position of the cylinders, how they go round, and the way in which one thing follows from another!"

Everyone said that they quite agreed, and the Master of Music got permission to show the bird to the public on the following Sunday. "They must also hear it sing," said the Emperor. And hear it they did. They were as delighted as if they had drunk themselves merry on tea and that's so like the Chinese! They all said "Oh!" and held up one finger – the finger we call "lick-pot" – and nodded their heads. But the poor fisherman who had heard the real nightingale said: "It don't sound so bad – quite like the bird – and yet there's something kind o' missing."

The real nightingale was sent into exile – banished from land and realm. The artificial bird had its place on a silk cushion close to the Emperor's bed; all the presents it had been given, gold and precious stones, lay round about, and it was promoted to be Chief Imperial Bedside Minstrel of the First Class on the Left; for the Emperor considered the side on which the heart lies to be the more distinguished, and even an Emperor has his heart on the left. The Master of Music wrote a book in twenty-five volumes about the mechanical bird; it was very long and learned, full of the most difficult Chinese words, and everyone pretended they had read it and understood it, or else of course they would have been thought stupid and got punched in the stomach.

Well, this went on for a whole year, until the Emperor, his Court and all the other Chinese knew by heart every little gurgle in the throat of the artificial songbird; but for that very reason they came to like it all the better. They could join in the singing themselves, and they did. The street-boys sang "zee-zee-zee, kloo-kloo-klook!" and the Emperor sang it, too! It really was tremendous fun.

But one evening, just as the artificial bird was in full song and the Emperor lay listening in bed, something went "snap!" inside the bird. Then there was a "whirrrr"; the wheels all went whizzing round … and the music stopped.

The Emperor jumped quickly out of bed and sent for the doctor, but what could he do? Then they brought along the watchmaker, and after a great deal of talk and poking about he got the bird to work after a fashion; but he said that it mustn't be used too often, as the bearings were almost worn out and it was impossible to get fresh parts that would fit in properly with the music. This was a sad disappointment. Once a year only was the artificial bird allowed to sing, and even that was something of a strain; but on these occasions the Master of Music made a little speech full of difficult words, saying that the bird was just as good as ever – and so of course it was just as good as ever.

Five years had now gone by and presently the whole country was filled with sorrow, for really in their hearts they were all fond of their Emperor; but now he was ill and not likely to live, it was said. A new Emperor had already been chosen, and people stood out in the street and asked the gentleman-in-waiting how their Emperor was. "P!" he replied and shook his head.

Cold and pale lay the Emperor in his magnificent great bed. The whole Court believed him to be dead, and each of them hastened to pay their respects to the new Emperor. The valets ran out to gossip about it, and the palace housemaids had a large tea-party. Everywhere, in all the rooms and corridors, heavy cloth had been laid down in order to deaden the sound of footsteps; the whole palace was as still as still could be.

But the Emperor wasn't dead yet. Stiff and pale he lay in the magnificent bed with its long velvet curtains and heavy gold tassels; through an open window high up on the wall the moon was shining down on the Emperor and the artificial bird.

The poor Emperor could scarcely breathe; it was just as if something was sitting on his chest. He opened his eyes, and then he saw it was Death that sat on his chest and had put on his gold crown and was holding the Emperor's gold sword in one hand and his splendid banner in the other. All round the bed, from the folds in the great velvet curtains, strange faces were peering, some of them hideous, others wonderfully gentle and kind. They were the Emperor's good and evil deeds gazing down on him now that Death was sitting on his heart.

"Do you remember that?" they whispered, one after the other. "Do you remember that?" And they told him so much that the sweat stood out on his forehead.

"I never realized that," said the Emperor. "Music, music! Sound the great Chinese drum," he cried, "to save me from hearing what they say!" But still they went on, and Death kept nodding like a Chinese at every word they whispered.

"Music! music!" shrieked the Emperor. "You wonderful little golden bird, sing, I implore you, sing! I've given you gold and precious stones, I've hung my own gold slipper round your neck – sing, I implore you, sing!"

But the bird was silent; there was no one to wind it up, and it couldn't sing without that. But Death went

on staring at the Emperor with his great hollow eyes, and everything was so still, so terribly still.

All at once, close to the window, came a burst of most beautiful singing. It was the little live nightingale, perched in a tree outside. She had heard of her Emperor's distress and had therefore come to sing him consolation and hope; and, as she sang, the shapes grew fainter and fainter, the blood in the Emperor's weak limbs ran faster and faster, and Death himself listened and said, "Go on, little nightingale, go on!"

"Yes, if you'll give me the fine gold sword... if you'll give me the splendid banner... if you'll give me the Emperor's crown!"

And Death gave up each treasure for a song, and still the nightingale went on singing. She sang of the quiet churchyard where the white roses bloom, where the elder-tree smells so sweet, and where the fresh grass is watered with the tears of those who are left behind. Then Death began to long for his garden and floated like a cold white mist out of the window.

"Thank you, thank you!" said the Emperor. "You heavenly little bird, now I know who you are! I banished you from land and realm – and yet you have sung those evil visions away from my bed, you have lifted Death from my heart. How can I ever repay you?"

"You have done already," said the nightingale. "The first time I sang I brought tears to your eyes – I shall never forget that. Those are the jewels that rejoice a singer's heart... But sleep now and get well and strong again! I will sing to you."

And the nightingale sang, and the Emperor fell into a sweet sleep – such a peaceful refreshing sleep. When he awoke, restored once more to health, the sun was shining in through the windows. None of his servants had come back yet, for they thought he was dead; but the nightingale was still singing outside.

"You must never leave me again," said the Emperor. "You shall only sing when you want to, and the artificial bird – I shall break it into a thousand pieces."

"No, don't do that," said the nightingale. "It's done what it could; don't part with it yet. I can't make my home in the palace, but let me come when I feel that I want to; then I'll sit of an evening on this branch by the window, and my singing can make you both gay and thoughtful. I shall sing of those that are happy, and of those that suffer; I shall sing of the good and the evil that are here lurking about you. Your little song-

bird must fly round to distant homes – to the poor fisherman and the humble peasant – to those who are far from you and your Court. I love your heart better than your crown... and yet there's a breath of something holy about the crown... I shall come, I shall sing to you; yet there's one thing you must promise me."

"Whatever you ask!" answered the Emperor, standing there in the imperial robes that he had himself put on and holding the heavy gold sword to his heart.

"One thing only I ask of you. Let no one know that you have a little bird who tells you everything; that will be best." And then the nightingale flew away.

The servants came in to look after their dead Emperor. Yes, there they stood, and the Emperor said, "Good morning!"

The Shepherdess and the Chimney-Sweep

Have you ever seen a real old-fashioned cupboard, its
wood quite black with age and carved all over with
twirls and twisting foliage? There was one just like that
in a certain sitting-room. It had been left by a great-
grandmother and was carved from top to bottom with
roses and tulips and the quaintest flourishes, and in
among were little stags poking out their heads that
were covered with antlers. But, carved on the middle
of the cupboard, was the complete figure of a man; he
really did look comic. And his grin was comic, too –
you couldn't call it a laugh – and he had billygoat legs,

little horns on his forehead and a long beard. The children who lived there always called him "Major-and-Minor-General-Company-Sergeant Billygoatlegs, because it was a difficult name to say, and there aren't many who get that rank. What a job it must have been to carve him out! Well, anyhow, there he was; and all the time he kept looking at the table under the looking-glass, for there stood a lovely little china shepherdess. She had gilt shoes, a frock that was charmingly caught up with a red rose, and a gold hat and shepherd's crook; she was delicious. Close beside her was a little chimney-sweep, as black as coal, though he too was made of china. He was just as trim and tidy as anyone else, for he really only pretended to be a chimney-sweep; the man who made him could just as well have made him a Prince, for that matter.

There he stood, looking so smart with his ladder and with cheeks as pink and white as a girl's. That was really a mistake; better if he'd been just a little bit sooty. He was standing quite close to the shepherdess; they had both been placed where they were and, because of that, they had become engaged. They certainly suited each other: they were both young, both made of the same china, and both equally brittle.

Near them, three times their size, was another figure – an old Chinaman who could nod. He too was made of porcelain, and he said he was the little shepherdess's grandfather, though he couldn't prove it. Still, he claimed to be her guardian; and so, when Major-and-Minor-General-Company-Sergeant Billygoatlegs had asked for the hand of the little shepherdess, the old Chinaman nodded his consent.

"There's a husband for you," he said; "a husband I'm almost sure is made of mahogany. He will make you Mrs. Major-and-Minor-General-Company-Sergeant Billygoatlegs. That cupboard of his is full of silver, to say nothing of what he has stowed away secretly."

"I won't go into that dark cupboard," said the little shepherdess. "I've heard that he's got eleven porcelain wives in there already."

"Then you can be the twelfth," said the Chinaman. "Tonight, as soon as ever the old cupboard starts creaking, you two shall be married – as sure as I'm a Chinese."And then with another nod he went off to sleep.

But the little shepherdess was in tears and looked at her darling sweetheart, the porcelain chimney-sweep. "I've something to ask you," she said. "Will you come with me out into the wide world? We can't possibly stay here."

"I'll do whatever you like," said the chimney-sweep. "Let's go at once; I feel sure I can earn enough at my job to support you."

"How I wish we were safely down from this table!" she said. "I shan't be happy till we're out in the wide world."

He did his best to console her, and he showed her how to put her little foot on the carved ledges and the gilded tracery that went winding round the leg of the table; and he also used his ladder to help her, and there they were at last on the floor. But when they looked across at the old cupboard, there was such a to-do. All the carved stags were poking out their heads and pricking up their antlers and twisting their necks. Major-and-Minor-General-Company-Sergeant Billygoatlegs jumped right up and shouted across to the old Chinaman, "Look! They're running away, they're running away!"

That gave them a bit of a scare, and they quickly popped into the drawer under the window-seat. They found three or four packs of cards in there, one of them complete, and a little toy-theatre that had been put together after a fashion. They were doing a play, and all the Queens – hearts and diamonds, clubs and spades – sat in the front row fanning themselves with their tulips, while behind them stood all the Knaves showing that they had heads both top and bottom, as they do on cards. The play was about a couple who weren't allowed to get married, and it made the shepherdess cry, because that was her story all over again.

"I can't bear it," she said. "I must get out of this drawer." But when they reached the floor and looked up at the table, the old Chinaman had woken up; his whole body was swaying to and fro, for, you see, the lower part of him was all one piece.

"Here comes the old Chinaman!" shrieked the little shepherdess, and she was in such a way that she sank down on her porcelain knees.

"I've got an idea," said the chimney-sweep. "Let's crawl down into the big pot-pourri jar over there in the corner; we can lie there on roses and lavender and throw salt in his eyes when he comes."

"That wouldn't be any good," she said. "Besides, I know the old Chinaman and the pot-pourri jar used to be engaged; and there's always a little tenderness left over, once people have been like that to each other. No, there's nothing for it but to go out into the wide world."

"Are you really as brave as that – to come out with me into the wide world?" asked the chimney-sweep. "Do you realize how huge it is, and that we can never come back here again?"

"I do," she answered.

Then the chimney-sweep looked her full in the face and said, "My way lies through the chimney. Are you really as brave as that – to crawl with me through the stove, past firebricks and flue, till we come out into the chimney? Once we're there, I know what I'm doing. We shall climb so high that they can't get at us, and right at the very top there's a hole leading out into the wide world."

And he led her up to the door of the stove.

"It does look black," she said; but she went with him all the same, past firebricks and flue, and where it was pitch-dark.

"Now we're in the chimney," he said, "and, look, there is the loveliest star shining overhead!"

Yes, it was a real star in the sky, shining straight down to them, just as though it wanted to show them the way. And they crawled and crept – it was a horrible climb – up and up. But he kept lifting and helping and holding her, pointing out the best places for her to put her little china feet. And at last they got right up to the top of the chimney and sat down on the edge, for they were tired out, and no wonder.

There was the sky with all its stars over-head, and the town with all its roofs below them. They could see round in every direction, far out into the world. The poor shepherdess had never imagined it was like that; she laid her little head on the chimney-sweep's shoulder and cried and cried till the gold ran from her sash.

"This is too much!" she said. "I can't bear it – the world's far too big. If only I were back on the little table under the looking-glass! I shall never be happy until I'm there again. I've come with you into the wide world; now I want you to take me home again, if you love me at all."

The chimney-sweep tried every argument. He reminded her of the old Chinaman and of Major-and-Minor-General-Company-Sergeant Billygoatlegs; but she sobbed so bitterly and kept kissing her little chimney-sweep, so that at last he had to give way to her, wrong as it was.

Then with great difficulty they crawled down the chimney again, crept through the flue and the firebricks – it wasn't at all nice – and there they stood in the dark stove, lurking behind the door so as to find out what was going on in the room. There wasn't a sound. They peeped out.. goodnesss gracious! there in the middle of the floor lay the old Chinaman. In trying to run after them he had fallen off the table and was lying there smashed into three fragments. The whole of his back had come off in a single piece, and his head had bowled away into a corner. Major-and-Minor-General-Company-Sergeant Billygoatlegs stood where he had always stood, in deept thought.

"How dreadful!" cried the litle shepherdess. "Old Grandpa's broken, and it's all our fault. I shall never get over it." And she wrung her tiny hands.

"He can still be riveted," said the chimney-sweep. "He can quite well be riveted. Now, don't get so worked up. When they've glued his back for him and given him a nice rivet in the neck, he'll be as good as new again and able to say all sorts of nasty things to us."

"Do you think so?" she said – and then they clambered up on to the table where they had been standing before.

"Well, here we are back where we started," said the chimney-sweep. "We might have saved ourselves all that trouble."

"I do wish we had old Grandpa safely riveted," said the shepherdess. "Do you think it'll be very expensive?"

He was mended all right. The family had his back glued, and he was given a nice rivet in the neck. He was as good as new – but he couldn't nod.

"You *have* become high and mighty since you got broken," said Major-and-Minor-General-Company-

Sergeant Billygoatlegs. "Yet I can't see that it's anything to be so proud of. Well – am I to have her, or am I not?"

It was touching to see how the chimney-sweep and the little shepherdess looked at the old Chinaman; they were so afraid he might nod. But he couldn't do that, and he didn't like to have to explain to a stranger that he had a rivet in his neck for good and all. So the porcelain couple stayed together; and they blessed Grandfather's rivet and went on loving each other until at last they got broken.

The Ugly Duckling

Summertime! How lovely it was out in the country, with the wheat standing yellow, the oats green, and the hay all stacked down in the grassy meadows! And there went the stork on his long red legs, chattering away in Egyptian, for he had learnt that language from his mother. The fields and meadows had large woods all around, and in the middle of the woods there were deep lakes.

Yes, it certainly was lovely out in the country. Bathed in sunshine stood an old manor-house with a deep moat round it, and growing out of the wall down by the water were huge dock-leaves; the biggest of them were so tall that little children could stand upright underneath. The place was as tangled and twisty as the densest forest, and here it was that a duck was sitting on her nest. It was time for her to hatch out her little ducklings, but it was such a long job that she was beginning to lose patience. She hardly ever had a visitor; the other ducks thought more of swimming about in the moat than of coming and sitting under a dockleaf just for the sake of a quack with her.

At last the eggs cracked open one after the other – "peep! peep!" – and all the yolks had come to life and were sticking out their heads.

"Quack, quack!" said the mother duck, and then the little ones scuttled out as quickly as they could, prying all round under the green leaves; and she let them do this as much as they liked, because green is so good for the eyes.

"Oh, how big the world is!" said the ducklings. And they certainly had much more room now than when they were lying in the egg.

"Do you suppose this is the whole world!" said their mother. "Why, it goes a long way past the other side of the garden, right into the parson's field; but I've never been as far as that. Well, you're all out now, I hope" – and she got up from her nest – "no, not all; the largest egg is still here. How ever long will it be? I can't bother about it much more." And she went on sitting again.

"Well, how's it going?" asked an old duck who came to pay a call.

"There's just this one egg that's taking such a time," said the sitting duck. "It simply won't break. But just look at the others – the loveliest ducklings I've ever seen. They all take after their father – the wretch! Why doesn't he come and see me?"

"Let's have a look at the egg which wont' crack," said the old duck. "I'll bet it's a turkey's egg. That's how I was bamboozled once. The little ones gave me no end of trouble, for they were afraid of the water – fancy that! – I just couldn't get them to go in. I quacked and clacked, but it was no good. Let's have a look at the egg ... Ay, that's turkey's egg, depend upon it! Let it be and teach the others to swim."

"I think I'll sit just a little while yet," said the duck. "I've been sitting so long that it won't hurt to sit a little longer."

"Please yourself!" said the old duck, and away she waddled.

At last the big egg cracked. There was a "peep! peep!" from the young one as he tumbled out, looking so large and ugly. The duck glanced at him and said: "My! what a huge great duckling that is! None of the others look a bit like that. Still, it's never a turkey-chick, I'll be bound... Well, we shall soon find out. He shall go into the water, if I have to kick him in myself!"

The next day the weather was gloriously fine, with sun shining on all the green dock-leaves. The mother duck with her whole family came down to the moat. Splash! into the water she jumped. "Quack, quack!" she said, and one after another the ducklings plomped in after her. The water closed over their heads, but they were up again in a moment and floated along so beautifully. Their legs worked of their own accord, and now the whole lot were in the water – even the ugly grey duckling joined in the swimming.

"It's no turkey, that's certain", said the duck. "Look how beautifully he uses his legs and how straight he holds himself. He's my own little one all right, and he's quite handsome, when you really come to look at him. quack, quack! Now, come along with me and let me show you the world and introduce you all to the barnyard, but mind and keep close to me, so that nobody steps on you; and keep a sharp look-out for the cat."

Then they made their way into the duckyard. There was a fearful noise going on, for there were two families fighting for an eel's head, and after all it was the cat that got it.

"You see! That's the way of the world," said the mother duck and licked her bill, for she too had fancied the eel's head. "Now then, where are your legs?" she said, "Look slippy and make a nice bow to the old duck over there. She's the most genteel of all these; she has Spanish blood, that's why she's so plump. And do you see that crimson rag she wears on one leg? It's extremely fine; it's the highest distinction any duck can win. It's as good as saying that there is no thought of getting rid of her; man and beast are to take notice! Look alive, and don't turn your toes in! A well-bred duckling turns its toes out, like father and mother … That's it. Now make a bow and say 'quack'!"

They all obeyed; but the other ducks round about looked at them and said out loud: "There! Now we've got to have that rabble as well – as if there weren't enough of us already! Ugh! What a sight that duckling is! We can't possibly put up with him" – and one duck immediately flew at him and bit him in the neck.

"Leave him alone," said the mother. "He's doing no one any harm."

"Yes, but he's so gawky and peculiar," said the one that had pecked him, "so he'll have to be squashed."

"What pretty children you have, my dear!" said the old duck with the rag on her leg. "All of them but one, who doesn't seem right. I only wish you could make him all over again."

"No question of that, my lady," said the ducklings' mother. "He's not pretty, but he's so good-tempered and he can swim just as well as the others – I daresay even a bit better. I fancy his looks will improve as he grows up, or maybe in time he'll grow down a little. He lay too long in the egg – that's why he isn't quite the right shape." And then she plucked his neck for him and smoothed out his feathers. "Anyhow, he's a drake, and so it doesn't matter so much," she added. "I feel sure he'll turn out pretty strong and be able to manage all right".

"The other ducklings are charming," said the old duck. "Make yourselves at home, my dears, and if you should find such a thing as an eel's head you may bring it to me."

And so they made themselves at home.

But the poor duckling who was the last out of the egg and looked so ugly got pecked and jostled and teased by ducks and hens alike. "The great gawk!" they all clucked. And the turkey, who was born with spurs and therefore thought himself an emperor, puffed up his feathers like a ship under full sail and went straight at him, and then he gobble-gobbled till he was quite red in the face. The poor duckling didn't know where to turn; he was terribly upset over being so ugly and the laughing-stock of the whole barnyard.

That's how it was the first day, and afterwards things grew worse and worse. The poor duckling got chivied about by all of them; even his own brothers and sisters treated him badly, and they kept saying: "If only the cat would get you, you ridiculous great guy!" And the mother herself wished he were far away. The ducks nipped him, the hens pecked him, and the maid who had to feed the poultry let fly at him with her foot.

After that, he ran away and fluttered over the hedge, and the little birds in the bushes grew frightened and flew into the air. "That's because I'm so ugly," thought the duckling and closed his eyes – and yet managed to get away. Eventually he came out to the great marsh where the wild-ducks lived and lay there all night, utterly tired and dispirited.

In the morning the wild-ducks flew up and looked at their new companion. "What ever are you?" they asked, and the duckling turned in every direction and bowed as well as he could.

"What a scarecrow you are!" said the wild-ducks,

"but that won't matter to us, as long as you don't marry into our family." Poor thing! He wasn't dreaming of getting married; all he wanted was to be allowed to stay quietly among the rushes and drink a little marsh-water. After he had been there for two whole days, two wild-geese came along – or rather two wild-ganders, for they were both males. It was not long since they were hatched; that's why they were so perky.

"Look here, my lad!" they began. "You are so ugly that we quite like you. Will you come in with us and migrate? Not far off, in another marsh, are some very nice young wild-geese, none of them married, who can quack beautifully. Here's a chance for you to make a hit, ugly as you are."

"Bang! bang!" suddenly echoed above them, and both the ganders fell down dead in the rushes, and the water became red with blood. "Bang! bang!" sounded once more, and flocks of wild-geese flew up from the rushes, so that immediately fresh shots rang out. A big shoot was on. The party lay ready all round the marsh; some even sat up in the trees on the branches that stretched right out over the rushes. Clouds of blue smoke drifted in among the dark trees and hung far over the water. Splashing through the mud came the gun-dogs, bending back reeds and rushes this way and that. It was terrifying for the poor duckling, who was just turning his head round to bury it under his wing when he suddenly found close beside him a fearsome great dog with lolling tongue and grim, glittering eyes. It lowered its muzzle right down to the duckling, bared its sharp teeth and – splash! it went off again without touching him.

The duckling gave a sigh of relief. "Thank goodness, I'm so ugly that even the dog doesn't fancy the taste of me." And he lay there quite still, while the shot pattered on the reeds and crack after crack was heard from the guns.

It was late in the day before everything was quiet again, but the poor duckling didn't dare to get up yet; he waited several hours longer before he took a look round and then made off from the marsh as fast as he could go. Over field and meadow he scuttled, but there was such a wind that he found it difficult to get along.

Towards evening he came up to a poor little farm-cottage; it was so broken-down that it hardly knew which way to fall, and so it remained standing. The wind whizzed so fiercely round the duckling that he had to sit on his tail so as not to be blown over. The wind grew worse and worse. Then he noticed that the door had come off one of its hinges and hung so much on the slant that he could slip into the house through the crack. And that's just what he did.

There was an old woman living here with her cat and her hen. The cat, whom she called Sonny, could arch its back and purr; it could even give out sparks, if you stroked its fur the wrong way. The hen had such short little legs that it was called Chickabiddy Short-legs; it was a very good layer, and the woman loved it like her own child.

Next morning they at once noticed the strange

duckling, and the cat started to purr and the hen to cluck. "Why, what's up?" said the woman, looking round. But her sight wasn't very good, and she took the duckling for a fat duck that had lost its way. "My! What a find!" she said. "I shall be able to have duck's eggs – as long as it isn't a drake! We must give it a trial."

And so the duckling was taken on trial for three weeks; but there was no sign of an egg. Now, the cat

was master in the house and the hen was mistress, and they always used to say "We and the world," because they fancied that they made up half the world – what's more, much the superior half of it. The duckling thought there might be two opinions about that, but the hen wouldn't hear of it.

"Can you lay eggs?" she asked.

"No."

"Well, then, hold your tongue, will you!"

And the cat asked: "Can you arch your back or purr or give out sparks?"

"No."

"Well, then, your opinion's not wanted, when sensible people are talking."

And the duckling sat in the corner, quite out of spirits. Then suddenly he remembered the fresh air and the sunshine, and he got such a curious longing to swim in the water that – he couldn't help it – he had to tell the hen.

"What's the matter with you?" she asked. "You haven't anything to do that's why you get these fancies. They'd soon go, if only you'd lay eggs or else purr."

"But it's so lovely to swim in the water", said the duckling; "so lovely to duck your head in it and dive down to the bottom."

"Most enjoyable, I'm sure," said the hen.

"You must have gone crazy. Ask the cat about it – I've never met any one as clever as he is – ask him if he's fond of swimming or diving! I say nothing of myself. Ask our old mistress, the wisest woman in the world! Do you suppose that she's keen on swimming and diving?"

"You don't understand me," said the duckling.

"Well, if we don't understand you, I should like to know who would. Surely you'll never try and make out you are wiser than the cat and the mistress – not to mention myself. Don't be silly, child! Give thanks to your Maker for all the kindness you have met with. Haven't you come to a nice warm room, where you have company that can teach you something? But you're just a stupid, and there's no fun in having you here. You may take my word for it – if I say unpleasant things to you, it's all for your good; that's just how you can tell which are your real friends. Only see that you lay eggs and learn how to purr or give out sparks!"

"I think I'll go out into the wide world," said the duckling.

"Yes, do," said the hen.

And so the duckling went off. He swam in the water; he dived down; but none of them would have anything to do with him because of his ugliness.

Autumn now set in. The leaves in the wood turned yellow and brown, the wind seized them and whirled them about, while the sky above had a frosty look. The clouds hung heavy with hail and snow, and the raven who perched on the fence kept squawking "ow! ow!" – he felt so cold. The very thought of it gave you the shivers. Yes, the poor duckling was certainly having a bad time.

One evening, when there was a lovely sunset, a whole flock of large handsome birds appeared out of the bushes. The duckling had never seen such beautiful birds, all glittering white with long graceful necks. They were swans. They gave the most extraordinary cry, spread out their magnificent long wings and flew from this cold country away to warmer lands and open lakes.

They mounted high, high up into the air, and the ugly little duckling felt so strange as he watched them. He turned round and round in the water like a wheel and craned his neck in their direction, letting out a cry so shrill and strange that it quite scared even himself. Ah! he could never forget those beautiful, fortunate birds; and directly they were lost to sight he dived right down to the bottom and, when he came up again, he was almost beside himself. He had no idea what the birds were called, nor where they were flying to, and yet they were dearer to him, than any he had ever known; he didn't envy them in the least – how could he ever dream of such loveliness for himself? He would be quite satisfied, if only the ducks would just put up with him, poor gawky-looking creature!

What a cold winter it was! The duckling had to keep swimming about in the water to prevent it freezing right up. But every night the pool he was swimming in grew smaller and smaller; then the ice froze so hard that you could hear it creaking. The duckling had to keep his feet moving all the time to prevent the water from closing up. At last he grew faint with exhaustion and lay quite still and finally froze fast in the ice.

Early next morning he was seen by a peasant who went out and broke the ice with his wooden clog and carried the duckling home to his wife. And there they revived him.

The children wanted to play with him, but the duckling was afraid they meant mischief and fluttered in panic right up into the milkbowl, so that the milk slopped over into the room. The woman screamed out and clapped her hands in the air, and then he flew into the butter-tub, and from there down into the flour-bin, and out of it again. Dear, dear, he did look an object! The woman screamed at him and hit at him with the tongs, and the children tumbled over each other trying to catch him – how they laughed and shouted!... It was a good thing the door was open; the duckling darted out into the bushes and sank down, dazed, in the new-fallen snow.

But it would be far too dismal to describe all the want and misery the duckling had to go through during that hard winter... He was sheltering among the reeds on the marsh, when the sun began to get warm again and the larks to sing; beautiful spring had arrived.

Then all at once he tried his wings; the whirr of them was louder than before, and they carried him swiftly away. Almost before he realized it, he found himself in a big garden with apple-trees in blossom and sweet-smelling lilac that dangled from long green

boughs right over the winding stream. Oh, it was so lovely here in all the freshness of spring! And straight ahead, out of the thicket, came three beautiful white swans, ruffling their feathers and floating so lightly on the water. The duckling recognized the splendid creatures and was overcome with a strange feeling of melancholy.

"I will fly across to them, those royal birds! They will peck me to death for daring, ugly as I am, to go near them. Never mind! Better to be killed by them than be nipped by the ducks, pecked by the hens, kicked by the girl who minds the poultry, and suffer hardship in winter." And he flew out on to the water and swam towards the beautiful swans. As they caught sight of him, they darted with ruffled feathers to meet him. "Yes, kill me, kill me!" cried the poor creature and bowed his head to the water awaiting death. But what did he see there in the clear stream? It was a reflection of himself that he saw in front of him, but no longer a clumsy greyish bird, ugly and unattractive – no, he was himself a swan!

It doesn't matter about being born in a duckyard, as long as you are hatched from a swan's egg.

He felt positively glad at having gone through so much hardship and want; it helped him to appreciate all the happiness and beauty that were there to welcome him... And the three great swans swam round and round and stroked him with their beaks.

Some little children came into the garden and threw bread and grain into the water, and the smallest one called out: "There's a new swan!" and the other children joined in with shouts of delight: "Yes, there's a new swan!" And they clapped their hands and danced about and ran to fetch father and mother. Bits of bread and cake were thrown into the water, and everyone said. "The new one is the prettiest – so young and handsome!" And the old swans bowed before him.

This made him feel quite shy, and he tucked his head away under his wing – he himself hardly knew why. He was too, too happy, but not a bit proud, for a good heart is never proud. He thought of how he had been despised and persecuted, and now he heard everybody saying that he was the loveliest of all lovely birds. And the lilacs bowed their branches to him right down to the water, and the sunshine felt so warm and kindly. Then he ruffled his feathers, raised his slender neck and rejoiced from his heart: "I never dreamed of so much happiness, when I was the ugly duckling."

The Gardener and The Squire

About four miles from the capital stood an old manor-house with thick walls, turrets and stepped gables. Here lived, though only in the summer, a rich noble-man and his wife; this house was the best and hand-somest of the various houses they owned. Outside, it looked as if it had only just been built, but inside it was as cosy and comfortable as possible. The family arms were carved in stone over the entrance, beautiful roses climbed round arms and oriel window, and a large grass lawn spread out in front of the house; there were may trees, both pink and white, and there were rare flowers even outside the greenhouse.

The squire had also a clever gardener; the flowers, the orchard and the kitchen-garden were a treat to see. Up against this part of the garden there was still some of the old original garden left with box hedges clipped in the shape of crowns and pyramids. Behind these stood two massive old trees which were nearly always leafless, and you might well suppose that a gale or a waterspout had spattered great lumps of manure over them; but every lump was a bird's nest.

Here, from time out of mind, a swarm of screaming rooks and crows had built; it was an absolute colony of birds, and the birds were the masters, the landed proprietors, the oldest family on the estate, the real lords of the manor. None of the people down below meant anything to them, but they put up with these crawling creatures in spite of their sometimes banging away with their guns, so that the birds got their spines tickled and each of them flew up with frightened cries of "Caw! Caw!"

The gardener often spoke to his master and mistress about cutting down the old trees; they didn't look well (he said) and, once they were gone, the place would most likely be rid of the screaming birds, which would go in search of new quarters. But the squire was unwilling to give up either the trees or the swarms of birds; they were something the manor couldn't be without, something from the old days, and these should not be altogether lost to mind.

"Those trees have now become the birds' inheritance. Let them keep it, my good Larsen."

Larsen was the gardener's name, but we needn't bother any more about that.

"My dear Larsen, haven't you enough room already? With your flower-garden, glasshouses, orchard and kitchen-garden?"

Yes, he had all these, and he tended and looked after them with great keenness and skill. His master and mistress admitted this, and yet they couldn't hide from him the fact that at other people's houses they often ate fruit or saw flowers that were better than anything in their own garden. The gardener was sorry to hear this, for he did his best that the best should be done. He was good at heart and good at his job.

One day the squire sent for him and told him, as friend and master, that, on the previous day, at the house of some distinguished friends, they had been given apples and pears so rich in juice and flavour that they and all the guests were filled with admiration. The fruit was obviously not home-grown, but it ought to be introduced into this country, if it could stand the climate. The fruit was known to have been bought in the town at the leading fruiterer's, and the gardener should go in and find out where these apples and pears had come from and then order cuttings.

The gardener knew the fruiterer well, for it was to him that he sold for the squire the surplus fruit growing in the manor garden.

So the gardener went to town and asked the fruiterer where he had got these apples and pears that were so much admired.

"They come from your own garden," said the fruiterer and showed him both apples and pears, which he soon recognised.

Dear me, how pleased the gardener was! He hurried to the squire and explained to him that both apples and pears came from his own garden.

The squire and his lady could simply not believe this. "It's not possible, Larsen. Can you produce a written assurance from the fruiterer?"

Yes, he could; and he brought along a written certificate.

"How very odd!" said the squire.

And now every day at the manor huge bowls of these magnificent apples and pears from their own garden appeared on the table. Bushels and barrels of the fruit were sent to friends in and out of town, and even abroad, bringing no end of pleasure. Still, they had to admit that of course there had been two unusually good summers for fruit-trees; these had done well all over the country.

Time passed. The squire and his wife went and dined at Court. The day after, the gardener was sent for by his master. At the royal table they had had melons so full of juice and flavour from their Majesties' greenhouse.

"You must go to the royal gardener, my good Larsen, and get us some of the seeds of these delicious melons."

"But the royal gardener got the seeds from us," said the gardener, quite delighted.

"Then the man has known how to improve the fruit in some way," answered the squire. "Every melon was excellent."

"Well, that does make me feel proud," said the gardener. "l must explain to you, sir: the royal gardener has had no luck this year with his melons, and when he saw how fine ours were and tasted them, he ordered three of these to be sent up to the castle."

"Larsen, don't tell me that those melons were out of our garden!"

"I fancy so," said the gardener; and he went to the royal gardener and got out of him a written certificate saying that the melons on the King's table had come from the manor.

This was indeed a surprise for the squire, and he made no secret of the incident, but showed people the certificate and even had melon sent out far and wide just as previously the cuttings had been.

Then news came back that the seeds were striking and setting admirably and the plant was called after the squire's manor, so that in this way its name could now be read in English, German and French. That was something never dreamed of before.

"I do hope the gardener won't begin to think too much of himself," said the squire.

But the gardener took it in a very different way. His great ambition now was to establish his name as one of the leading gardeners in the country, and to try every year to produce something first-rate in gardening; and he did this. But, all the same, he often heard it said that his very first fruit, the apples and the pears, were really his best; all that came after was much inferior. The melons were no doubt extremely good, but they were of course something quite different. His strawberries might be called excellent, and yet no better than those to be found on other estates; and when one year the radishes were a failure, it was only the unfortunate radishes that they talked about and not a word about anything else that turned out well.

It was almost as though the squire felt relieved to be able to say, "Well, Larsen, rather a poor year, eh?" They quite enjoyed saying, "Rather a poor year."

Twice a week the gardener brought fresh flowers up

to the house, always most tastefully arranged. The colours seemed to be heightened by the way they were grouped.

"You have taste, Larsen," said the squire. "That's a gift, not of your own, but of God."

One day the gardener brought in a big crystal bowl the leaf of a water-lily lying inside. On this had been laid, with its long thick stalk down in the water, a brilliant blue flower as large as a sunflower.

"An Indian water-lily!" exclaimed the squire and his wife. They had never seen such a flower; by day it was carefully placed in the sun and, when evening came, in a reflected light. Everyone who saw it thought it very lovely and most unusual; even the highest young lady in the land said so, and she was a princess, kind and sensible.

The squire and his lady were only too proud to present her with the flower, and she took it with her back to the castle. Then they both went down into the garden to pick a similar flower themselves, if such a thing was still to be found; but it wasn't. So they called the gardener and asked him where he'd got the blue water-lily from.

"We can't find it anywhere," they said. "We've been through the green-houses and right round the flower-garden."

"Well, but that's not where it is," said the gardener. "It's only a humble flower from the kitchen-garden. Still, it is beautiful, isn't it? It looks like a blue cactus, and yet it's only the blossom on an artichoke."

"You should have told us that straight away," said the squire. "We couldn't help thinking it was a rare foreign flower. You've made us look ridiculous in the eyes of the young Princess. She saw the flower at our house and found it so beautiful. She didn't know what it was – though she's well up in botany – but that science has nothing to do with vegetables. How on earth, my good Larsen, could you think of sending such a flower up to the house? It will make us a laughing-stock."

And the pretty blue flower that had been brought from the kitchen-garden was taken away from the room at the manor, where it was quite out of place; and the squire sent an excuse to the Princess, explaining that the flower was nothing but a vegetable which the gardener had taken into his head to display, and for this he had had a good talking-to.

"What a shame! How unfair!" said the Princess. "Why, he has opened our eyes to a splendid flower we had never noticed; he has shown us beauty where we never dreamed of looking. Every day, as long as the artichokes are in flower, the royal gardener is to bring me one up to my room."

And this was done.

The squire sent word to the gardener that he might again bring them a fresh artichoke blossom.

"It's really quite handsome," he said; "altogether remarkable." And the gardener was praised.

"That's what Larsen enjoys," said the squire. "He's a spoilt child."

In the autumn there was a tremendous gale. It sprang up in the small hours and was so violent that numbers of big trees on the fringe of the wood were torn up by the roots, and to the great sorrow of the squire and his wife – sorrow for them, but joy for the gardener – the two massive trees were blown down, together with all the bird's-nests. The cries of rooks and crows could be heard through the gale, as they beat their wings on the windows, said the servants at the manor.

"Now, Larsen, I suppose you're happy," said the squire. "The gale has brought down the trees, and the birds have taken to the woods. So it's good-bye to the dear old days; not a sign or hint of them is left. To us it is a great grief."

The gardener said nothing – but he thought of what he had long had in mind – how he could best make use of the fine sunny space he had never before had at his disposal. It should grow to be an ornament to the garden and a joy to the squire.

The big trees that had been blown down had crushed and flattened the venerable boxhedges with all their cut-out patterns. Here he put up a thicket of shrubs, native plants from field and wood. Things that no other gardener had thought of putting in at all abundantly in the garden near the house, he now planted in their proper soil and in the shade and sunshine required by each sort. He tended in love, and they grew into splendour.

Junipers from the heaths of Jutland were raised, with

the shape and colour of Italy's cypress; the glossy prickly holly, green alike in winter cold or in summer sunshine, was a delight to the eye. In front grew ferns of every species, some looking as if they were children of the palm tree, and others as if they were parents of that lovely delicate plant we call maidenhair. Here was the despised burdock that when freshly picked is so beautiful that it can look fine in a bunch of flowers. The burdock was on dry soil, but on lower damper ground there grew the common dock, also a despised plant and yet with its height and its tremendous leaf wonderfully picturesque. Six foot high, with flower upon flower like a huge many-branched candlestick, rose the great mullein, transplanted from the fields. And here were sweet woodruff, primroses and lilies-of-the-valley, arum lilies and the delicate three-leaved wood sorrel... All most beautiful to look at.

In front, with steel wire supports, there grew rows of little French pear trees; they got plenty of sun and attention, and they soon bore large juicy pears, as they had done in the country they came from.

To take the place of the two old leafless trees, a tall flagstaff was put up flying the Danish flag, and, near by, another pole round which the hops twined their sweet-smelling clusters in summer and at harvest-time. But in winter according to ancient custom a sheaf of oats was hung from this pole, so that the birds of the air might have something to eat at happy Christmas time.

"Our good Larsen is getting sentimental in his old

age," said the squire. "But he's faithful and devoted to us."

With the New Year there appeared in one of the capital's illustrated papers a picture of the old manor-house, showing the flagstaff and the sheaf of oats for the birds at Christmas, and emphasis was laid on the happy idea of keeping up a time-honoured custom in this way – an idea so very characteristic of the old place.

"They beat the big drum for every mortal thing that Larsen does," said the squire. "He's a lucky man. I suppose we ought almost to be proud of having him."

But they weren't in the least proud of it. They felt that they were the master and mistress and could give Larsen a month's notice if they liked, but they didn't do that. They were kind people, and there are so many kind people of that sort. What a good thing that is for all the Larsens!

Well, that's the story of *The Gardener and the Squire*... Now you can think it over.

The Snow Man

Ooh! I'm creaking all over in this lovely cold weather," said the snow man. I must say the wind knows how to sting life into you. And that goggle-eye over there – how she does stare!" – it was the sun he meant, which was just going down – "she won't get me to wince; I can hold on to my bits all right." These were two large three-cornered bits of roof-tiles that he had for eyes; the mouth was part of an old rake, and so he had teeth.

He had been born amid shouts of glee from the boys, and saluted with jingling of bells and cracking of whips from the sledges.

The sun went down and the full moon rose, round and huge, clear and lovely in the blue sky. "There she comes again from another direction," said the snow man. He imagined it was the sun appearing once more. "I have cured her of staring. Now she can hang there and light me up to see myself. If I only knew how one sets about moving! I should so like to move. If I could, I would go straight away and do some sliding on the ice, as I saw the boys doing. But I don't know how to run."

"Be-off-off!" barked the old watchdog from his chain. He was a bit husky; he had been like that ever since he had lived indoors and lay close to the fire. "The sun will teach you to run all right! I saw that happen last year to the snow man before you, to the one before him, 'be-off-off' - and off they've gone."

"I don't follow you, mate," said the snow man. "Will that creature up there teach me how to run?" (He was referring to the moon.) "Well, yes, she ran fast enough just now, when I stared back at her; now she's creeping up from another direction."

"You don't know a thing," said the watchdog; "but, there, they've only just stuck you up. What you're looking at is called the moon; the other, who disappeared, was the sun. She'll come back tomorrow and show you well enough how to run – right down into the pond. There'll soon be a change in the weather, I can feel it in my left hind leg – such twinges! yes, the weather's going to change."

"I can't make him out," said the snow man, "though I've a feeling that it's something unpleasant he's getting at. The one who stared and went down – he calls her the sun – she isn't my friend either, I feel sure of that."

"Be-off-off!" barked the watchdog, turned round three times about himself and lay down inside his kennel to sleep.

There really was a change in the weather. A thick clammy fog settled down in the early morning over the whole neighbourhood. At break of day there was a light breeze; the wind was so icy cold that the frost got a firm grip. But what a sight there was when the sun rose! All the trees and bushes were covered with hoar-frost; it was like a whole forest of white coral; it was as if all the boughs had been smothered with glittering white blossoms. Thousands of delicate twigs, that in summer are not to be seen because of all the leaves, now stood out, every one of them. It all looked just like lace and so dazzling white that a white radiance appeared to stream from every branch. The weeping birch stirred in the breeze, with life in it you might see

in a tree in summer. You never saw such loveliness; and as the sun shone out, goodness! how everything sparkled as if it had been sprinkled over with diamond dust, and the whole snow-covered earth was a glitter of big diamonds – or you might also suppose they were thousands of tiny candles, even whiter than the snow itself.

"How perfectly beautiful!" said a girl, as she stepped with a young man out into the garden and paused alongside the snow man, looking at the glistening trees. "You couldn't see anything lovelier even in summer," she said with sparkling eyes.

"Nor a fellow like this one here – you'd never come

across him," said the young man and pointed at the snow man. "He's splendid!"

The girl laughed and gave the snow man a nod; then she tripped off with her friend across the snow, which crunched under them as if they were walking on starch.

"Who were those two?" the snow man asked the watchdog. "You've been here longer than I have; do you know them?"

"Indeed I do," replied the watchdog. "She sometimes pats my back, and he has given me a bone. I'll never bite *them*."

"But what are they doing here?" asked the snow man.

"They're swee-eethearts!" said the watchdog. "They are to move into a kennel of their own and gnaw bones together. Be-off-off!"

"Are these two just as important as you and I?" asked the snow man.

"Well, you see, they belong to the family," said the

watchdog. "It's true, no one can be expected to know much if he was born yesterday. That's clearly the case with you. Now, I possess age and knowledge; I know everyone here at the house. There was a time when I didn't have to stand chained up here in the cold. Be-off-off!"

"But cold is delightful," said the snow man. "Do go on with your story! But don't keep rattling your chain; that upsets me."

"Be-off-off!" barked the watchdog. "I was a puppy then; a sweet little thing, they said I was. There I lay indoors on a velvet chair, curled up on my lady's lap. I was kissed on the nose and had my paws wiped with an embroidered handkerchief; they called me "the beautifullest", "ducky-ducky-darling"... But soon I grew too big for them, and they gave me to the housekeeper. I came down to the basement; you can see into it from where you're standing. You can see down into the room where I was lord and master, for that's what I was with the housekeeper. I dare say they were humbler quarters than upstairs, but it was more comfortable here: I wasn't pawed and lugged about by children as I had been upstairs. I got just as good food as before, and much more of it. I had my own cushion, and then there was a stove. That's the most glorious thing in the world at this time of the year. I used to crawl right in underneath it, till I was out of sight. Oh, I still dream of that stove. Be-off-off!"

"Is a stove really so nice to look at?" asked the snow man. "Is it at all like me?"

"It's just the opposite of you. Coal-black, and has a long neck with brass collar. It feeds on logs, so that flames shoot out of its mouth. You can keep beside it, close up, or right under; it is such a comfort. You must be able to see it through the window from where you are."

And the snow man looked and, sure enough, he saw a shiny black-polished object with a brass collar; fire was gleaming out from below. The snow man had a strange sensation, a feeling he couldn't himself account for. Something came over him that was quite new to him, though people all know it who are not snow men.

"And why did you leave her?" asked the snow man, for he felt that the stove must be one of the female sex. "How could you desert such a spot?"

"Well, the fact is I had to," said the watchdog. "They turned me out and chained me up here. I had bitten the youngest son of the house in the leg, because he had kicked away the bone I was gnawing; a bone for a bone, I thought. But they didn't like it, and from that day I've been chained up and have lost my clear voice; listen how hoarse I am – be-off-off! That was the end of it all."

The snow man gave up listening. He still went on staring into the housekeeper's basement, down into her room where the stove stood on its four iron legs and looked about the size of the snow man himself.

"There's a queer creaking inside me," he said. "Am I never to come into that room? It's an innocent wish,

and surely our innocent wishes ought to be granted. It's my greatest wish, my one and only wish; and it would be hardly fair if it weren't satisfied. I must come in, I must nestle up against her, even if I have to smash the window."

"You'll never come in there," said the watchdog; and if you did reach the stove you'd soon be off, off!"

"I'm as good as off already," said the snow man. "I feel I'm breaking up."

All day long the snow man stood looking in at the window. At dusk the room became still more inviting. The stove shone so kindly in a way that neither moon nor sun can ever shine – no, but as only a stove can shine, when there's something in it. When the door was opened, the flame shot out; that was its habit. The snow man's white face went flaming red, and the pink glow spread right up his chest.

"It's more than I can bear," he said. "How pretty she looks when she puts out her tongue!"

The night was very long, but not for the snow man. He stood there with his own beautiful thoughts, and they froze till they crackled. In the early morning the basement windows were frozen over; they had the loveliest ice-ferns any snow man could ask for, but they hid the stove. The panes refused to thaw, so he couldn't see her. There was crackling and crunching, it was exactly the kind of frosty weather to delight a snow man; but he was not delighted. He might and ought to have felt so happy, but he wasn't happy; he had 'stove-sickness'.

"That's a serious complaint for a snow man," said the watchdog, "I've had it myself, but I've got over it – be-off-off! There's a change in the weather coming."

And there was a change in the weather; it turned to a thaw. The thaw increased, the snow man decreased. He didn't say anything, he didn't complain, and that's a sure sign.

One morning he collapsed. Where he had been standing there was something like a broom-handle sticking out; it was round this the boys had built him up.

"Now I understand about his 'stove-sickness'," said the watchdog. "The snow man has a stove-rake in his body; that's what upset him, and now he's done with it. Be-off-off!"

And soon winter was done with too.

"Be-off-off!" barked the watchdog; but the little girls at the house sang:

"Sweet woodruff, now's the time to sprout,
and, willow, hang your mittens out.
Come, lark, and cuckoo, when you sing
then winter's gone and here is spring.
I'll join you both – twit-twit! cuckoo!
Come, darling sun, we long for you!"

After that, nobody gave a thought to the snow man.

The little Match-Seller

It was terribly cold. Snow was falling and soon it would be quite dark; for it was the last day in the year – New Year's Eve. Along the street, in that same cold and dark, went a poor little girl in bare feet – well, yes, it's true, she had slippers on when she left home; but what was the good of that? They were great big slippers which her mother used to wear, so you can imagine the size of them; and they both came off when the little girl scurried across the road just as two carts went whizzing by at a fearful rate. One slipper was not to be found, and a boy ran off with the other, saying it would do for a cradle one day when he had children of his own.

So there was the little girl walking along in her bare

feet that were simply blue with cold. In an old apron she was carrying a whole lot of matches, and she had one bunch of them in her hand. She hadn't sold anything all day, and no one had given her a single penny. Poor mite, she looked so downcast as she trudged along hungry and shivering. The snowflakes settled on her long flaxen hair, which hung in pretty curls over her shoulder; but you may be sure she wasn't thinking about her looks. Lights were shining in every window, and out into the street came the lovely smell of roast goose. You see, it was New Year's Eve; that's what she was thinking about.

Over in a little corner between two houses – one of them jutted out rather more into the street than the other – there she crouched and huddled with her legs tucked under her; but she only got colder and colder. She didn't dare to go home, for she hadn't sold a match nor earned a single penny. Her father would beat her, and besides it was so cold at home. They had only the bare roof over their heads and the wind whistled through that although the worst cracks had been stopped up with rags and straw. Her hands were really quite numb with cold. Ah, but a little match – that would be a comfort. If only she dared pull one out of the bunch, just one, strike it on the wall and warm her fingers! She pulled one out... ritch!... how it spirted and blazed! Such a clear warm flame, like a little candle, as she put her hand round it – yes, and what a curious light it was! The little girl fancied she was sitting in front of a big iron stove with shiny brass knobs and brass facings, with such a warm friendly fire burning... why, whatever was that? She was just stretching out her toes, so as to warm them too, when – out went the flame, and the stove vanished. There she sat with a little stub of burnt-out match in her hand.

She struck another one. It burned up so brightly, and where the gleam fell on the wall this became transparent like gauze. She could see right into the room, where the table was laid with a glittering white cloth and with delicate china; and there, steaming deliciously, was the roast goose stuffed with prunes and apples. Then, what was even finer, the goose jumped off the dish and waddled along the floor with the carvingknife and fork in its back. Right up to the poor little girl it came... but then the match went out, and nothing could be seen but the massive cold wall.

She lighted another match. Now she was sitting under the loveliest Christmas tree; it was even bigger and prettier than the one she had seen through the glass-door at the rich merchant's at Christmas. Hundreds of candles were burning on the green branches, and gay-coloured prints, like the ones they hang in the shop-windows, looked down at her. The little girl reached up both her hands … then the match went out; all the Christmas candles rose higher and higher, until now she could see they were the shining stars. One of them rushed down the sky with a long fiery streak.

"That's somebody dying," said the little girl, for her

dead Grannie, who was the only one who had been kind to her, had told her that a falling star shows that a soul is going up to God.

She struck yet another match on the wall. It gave a glow all around, and there in the midst of it stood her old grandmother, looking so very bright and gentle and loving. "Oh, Grannie", cried the little girl, "do take me with you! I know you'll disappear as soon as the match goes out – just as the warm stove did, and the lovely roast goose, and the wonderful great Christmas-tree". And she quickly struck the rest of the matches in the bunch, for she did so want to keep her Grannie there. And the matches flared up so gloriously that it became brighter than broad daylight. Never had Grannie looked so tall and beautiful. She took the little girl into her arms, and together they flew in joy and splendour, up, up, to where there was no cold, no hunger, no fear. They were with God.

But in the cold early morning huddled between the two houses, sat the little girl with rosy cheeks and a smile on her lips, frozen to death on the last night of the old year. The New Year dawned on the little dead body leaning there with the matches, one lot of them nearly all used up. "She was trying to get warm," people said. Nobody knew what lovely things she had seen and in what glory she had gone with her old Grannie to the happiness of the New Year.